Captains of the City Streets

Other Books About the Cat Club by Esther Averill

THE CAT CLUB

THE SCHOOL FOR CATS

JENNY'S FIRST PARTY

JENNY'S MOONLIGHT ADVENTURE

WHEN JENNY LOST HER SCARF

JENNY'S ADOPTED BROTHERS

HOW THE BROTHERS JOINED THE
CAT CLUB

JENNY'S BIRTHDAY BOOK

JENNY GOES TO SEA

JENNY'S BEDSIDE BOOK

THE FIRE CAT (An I CAN READ Book)

THE HOTEL CAT

Captains of the City Streets
A Story of the Cat Club

written and illustrated
by Esther Averill

A HARPER TROPHY BOOK

Harper & Row, Publishers
New York, Evanston, San Francisco, London

CAPTAINS OF THE CITY STREETS

Copyright © 1972 by Esther Averill

Standard Book Number: 06–440070–0

First printed in 1972.
2nd printing, 1973.
First Trophy edition.

CONTENTS

At The Tramps' Last Stop   1

The House of Their Own   22

A Strange Sight in Another Garden   44

A Closer View of the Cat Club   59

Face to Face with the President   76

Little Mac   85

In the Visitors' Row   95

Three Nights of Rain   108

Captains of the City Streets   116

Another Talk with Patchy Pete   136

At The Tramps'
Last Stop

It was a night in early spring. The moon shone bright in a starry sky. And below, in the city, a pair of raggedy young cats trudged wearily down the sidewalk of the last block of the broad highway. They were the tramp cats, Sinbad and The Duke.

Sinbad and The Duke were thin and bony, big young cats. Their darkish fur was speckled by rough weather. Sinbad had a yellow ear and a spiky tail. Except for this

1

ear and the tail, these tramps looked much alike.

Sinbad and The Duke were much alike in other respects. Both cats had been born and raised here in New York City, and together they had planned this journey. They had set forth on the journey together and had stuck together through thick and thin. And all the long while they had continued to share the high hope of the journey's final success.

Right now they were hungry—so hungry that they could think of nothing but something to eat. Thus, when they came to the square where the broad highway and its roaring traffic ended, they walked around

2

the square to the south side. There they found the narrow street on whose corner stood the restaurant known in the cat world as The Tramps' Last Stop. Sinbad and The Duke had heard from other tramps that at this eating place a cat was sure to get a handout. Handouts were those gifts of food supplied to tramps by kindly humans. Handouts helped to keep alive the homeless cats of the city.

Sinbad and The Duke peered cautiously into the backyard of The Tramps' Last Stop. They used caution because experience

had taught them that four-footed creatures adrift in the big city should watch out for danger. No danger could be detected in the backyard of this restaurant. It was a small yard, filled with moonlight and shadows. After the beat and bustle of the highway along which the young tramps had been traveling, the place seemed like a pool of quiet.

Across the yard, in the shadow of a wall, sat three other cats—old tramps who kept the peaceful silence, which was broken only by the rattle of the kitchen's pots and pans.

One of the old tramps called out to Sinbad and The Duke: "Hi, young fellas! Come and sit with us. Then Cookie'll be sure to see you're here."

The old tramp had a pleasant voice. It was the voice of one who could be trusted. Sinbad and The Duke walked over and seated themselves beside him. His fur was a coat of many colors.

"My name is Patchy Pete," said he.

"I'm Sinbad," said the young one with the yellow ear and the spiky tail.

"I'm The Duke," said his companion.

"Your first visit to this place?" queried Patchy Pete.

"Yes," they answered.

Patchy Pete said, "It's worth the trip. No finer cook in all New York than Cookie. And tonight it's chicken à la king."

"Wow!" said Sinbad and The Duke. And they sniffed the air, smelled the chickeny smell, and felt too hungry to carry on the conversation.

All five cats now sat in silence, while each waited for the handout which would be given him after the humans in the front of the restaurant had been fed.

Presently the kitchen door was opened, and in the lighted doorway appeared a jolly-looking man who wore a white apron and a tall white cap. He glanced at the silent, waiting cats, as if to count their noses. Then he disappeared behind the closed door of the kitchen.

Patchy Pete said to Sinbad and The Duke, "That was Cookie. No kinder human anywhere. And none more understanding of us tramps. He won't take any thanks for his handouts. He doesn't even give us any chance to thank him. He just lets us eat in peace and then go in peace to wherever we're going."

The old tramp gazed at the young ones to see if they wished to tell him where they themselves might be going from there. But as they could think only of their supper, they said nothing.

A few minutes later, Cookie came into the yard. He walked softly and carried a big tray which gave forth the delicious smell of chicken à la king. But he did not go near the tramps. Instead, he set the contents of the tray on the ground in another part of the yard. Then he returned to the kitchen and quietly shut the door.

"Suppertime," announced the old tramp of the many-colored coat.

Sinbad and The Duke followed Patchy Pete to the supper ground. So did the other two old tramps, who had not spoken. Those two seemed to be the silent kind. Even their dull coats, one of which was grey and the other reddish, looked like the coats of silent cats.

On the supper ground were five saucers heaped with chicken à la king—a separate saucer for each customer. Sinbad and The Duke gobbled their chicken à la king, licked their saucers clean, and were then ready for some drinks. But the five customers were supposed to share the milk, which had been

7

provided in one big bowl, and the water, which stood in a smaller one. Sinbad and The Duke, out of courtesy, were obliged to wait and give the older cats first chance at the drinking bowls.

The three oldsters ate slowly, as if they'd lost some of their teeth. But the grey tramp and the reddish one eventually finished their eating and drinking. Then, silently and separately, they walked out of the yard. Sinbad and The Duke had often seen the likes of them. Such tramps were the broken-hearted ones, the real loners.

Sinbad and The Duke were not real loners. They lived by themselves, but they had each other. They were buddies.

They'd been buddies ever since last winter, when they met for the first time in a deserted cellar, where each had taken refuge from the wind and snow. Each of them, at that time, was homeless. For each had lost a beloved master through death, and afterward there had been no human to take care of them. Each had consequently fend for himself, all by himself, on the streets. Happy was Sinbad, happy was the Duke at that first glimpse of one another in that deserted cellar. There they became buddies and swore never to part.

After they became buddies, Sinbad and The Duke had traveled together from neighborhood to neighborhood and lived chiefly on modest handouts. Tonight's chicken à la king had been a rare treat. It had also restored their strength. They now felt inclined to talk with Patchy Pete, who was still busy with his supper. He looked like a tramp who had seen the world. And since he seemed to be a pleasant soul, maybe they could get from him some helpful information about where they planned to go from there.

The old tramp at last finished his food and drinks and gazed at the raggedy young ones. He said to them in his pleasant, rusty voice, "Your turn now at the drinking bowls. Take your time. I'll wait for you. A little conversation after a feast like this adds to the evening's pleasure."

Sinbad and The Duke drank their fill of milk, lapped some water, and then were ready for Patchy Pete to open the conversation.

"Buddies, I take it," he began.

"Yes, we travel together," they answered in the single voice which they often used when there was no need for them to speak separately.

"Ah," said Patchy Pete, "there's nothing like a buddy. I myself once had one. Then, woe is me, I lost him, killed by a car. So now I travel alone. But I've learned to find company in the strange sights that meet my eyes

strange stories that befall my ears.
o fellas have aroused my interest.
ook like young tramps with a future.
ither bound?"

"To the south part of the city," they said.

"To the south part!" exclaimed Patchy Pete. "By the pads of my paws, the south part is no place for you. Don't you know why this restaurant is called The Tramps' Last Stop? Don't you know that it's really the last point on the city's north-south route where a cat may be sure of a handout?"

"So we've heard," admitted the buddies.

"Then why go south?" asked Patchy Pete.

Sinbad answered, "We spent last winter in the north part of the city and had a terrible time."

The Duke added, "The buildings were so high we couldn't see the tops of them and so close together we couldn't squeeze our way between them."

And the buddies in their single voice said, "Worst of all, we were driven from cellar to

cellar. Couldn't rest our legs for two nights in the same spot."

"But, fellas," said Patchy Pete, "even in the north part, which has those big, new buildings, there are handouts. Not so many handouts as there used to be, yet still a few, whereas the south part of the city has long been called 'the land of no handouts.'"

"Just the same," replied the buddies, "we'd rather go to the south part."

"The east part would be better," observed Patchy Pete. "You would find handouts in the east part and also in the west part. I'm heading westward myself tonight, for I feel a pull toward the city's docks and the sight of the ships that come in from the sea. And by the docks there's a little restaurant that serves bluefish."

"Patchy Pete, the south part's where we'd like to go," they insisted.

"Why?" demanded the old tramp.

"Because," said they, "we've heard that of all New York City the south part's the best place to find what we're looking for."

"What in the world are you after?" he asked.

"A house of our own," declared the buddies.

"A house of your own!" exclaimed Patchy Pete. "Skin me alive if I've ever heard of such a thing for tramps. And strong young fellas like yourselves. And in the springtime, when you could take to the open road and walk north, east, or west, with the sun and the moon on your spines, and make the most of your freedom. What's the matter with you? Are you growing soft?"

At the word "soft," Sinbad raised a big front paw and drove a hard right hook to The Duke's jaw. The Duke raised a big front paw and delivered a similar hard hook to Sinbad's jaw. Then the buddies exchanged

jabs and punches until Patchy Pete called, "Enough! Your boxing proves that you aren't softies. Your front-paw work is powerful. But you must practice your skips and shuffles."

"Patchy Pete, that's why we're going

southward—to find a little house where we can practice our skips and shuffles."

The old tramp scratched his ear, as if he needed time in which to think. Then he said in his kindly voice, "I don't like to put fleas in your dreams. But I went southward myself last fall to see what I could see. I feel I ought to tell you fellas what I saw. For I suppose that what I saw down there last fall is still pretty much the same this spring."

"Tell us about the buildings," they urged.

Patchy Pete replied, "It's true that just south of The Tramps' Last Stop lies a stretch of territory known in cat history as Little Old New York. Little Old New York is quite different from the rest of the city, where the buildings are bigger and newer. In Little Old New York the humans live in small, ancient houses of brick, and scattered among the houses are gardens that often have smaller, wooden buildings, such as sheds and deserted shacks."

"A shack! A cat-size shack! That's what we want," cried the buddies.

"But, fellas, I've already warned you that Little Old New York does not seem to welcome cats."

"Why doesn't it?" they asked.

Patchy Pete replied, "There's an old story, a legend, that tells how once upon a time many cats lived in Little Old New York. But some of them did mischief. Whereupon they and the rest of our tribe were driven out by the humans. Yes, driven out with sticks and stones."

"Don't any of us live there now?"

"I guess not," answered Patchy Pete. "Or rather, let me say that last fall, when I was there, Little Old New York seemed to be truly a catless land. I found no sign of any cat—either of an indoors cat or of a tramp —and not a single handout."

"How was the stealing?" asked the buddies.

"I found a number of small food shops that had easy-to-push-open doors."

"We'll live by stealing," they declared.

"But, fellas, you can't expect to go on stealing in the same neighborhood forever. Someday the humans may rise against you and drive you out with sticks and stones."

The buddies said, "We'll run faster than the sticks and stones, and get back safe to our little house and go on living there and boxing there and doing as we please to please ourselves."

The old tramp of the many-colored coat gave a snort. "Maybe," he said. "Maybe you'll find your dream house. Maybe you'll manage to live by stealing and not get driven out with sticks and stones. But wither my whiskers, if you'll be able to go on doing always as you please to please yourselves. You'll have lost your freedom."

"Why?" they demanded.

"Because," said the old tramp, "if you settle down in a house of your own, you'll become a part of your neighborhood. Then little duties toward your neighbors will arise. I can't imagine what those duties would be in your case. So let's just call them neighborhood obligations which you would have to fulfill."

"We won't let ourselves be trapped by any neighborhood obligations," vowed the buddies.

"Never say I didn't warn you," said Patchy Pete. "But I suppose young fellas like you must learn for yourselves and work things out for yourselves. And who am I to know how it will end? So now I'll tell you what you really want to hear."

"Yes," they begged, "tell us the best spot to hunt for our little house."

He said, "Go straight south from The Tramps' Last Stop until you come to a children's playground. Then go west until you come to a firehouse. It's the firehouse of the oldest part of Little Old New York. In this oldest part, a few blocks south of the firehouse, you will find the most comfortable deserted shacks and the food shops that have the easiest-to-push-open doors."

"Thanks for giving us the information," said the buddies.

"The pleasure was mine," replied Patchy Pete, using the courteous expression that was still favored by old-fashioned tramps. Then he gazed at the moon and rose to his feet, saying, "The hour is late. It's time for me to take to the open road."

"We'll go with you to the corner of the block," they told him.

Sinbad and The Duke accompanied Patchy Pete from the backyard of The Tramps' Last Stop to the street corner. There they said to him, "After we get settled in our little house, you must come and visit us."

"I have much traveling to do before I ever come. My thanks, though, for the invitation," he replied.

The old tramp of the many-colored coat walked westward into the night. But before he disappeared from view, he called back in his pleasant, rusty voice, "Happy boxing in your little house. And good luck with your neighborhood obligations."

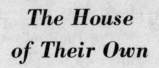

The House of Their Own

From The Tramps' Last Stop,
Sinbad and The Duke headed
southward through Little Old
New York. They were eager,

of course, to find a shack where they could make their permanent home. But they traveled only by night.

"Daytime's too dangerous," they reasoned. "We might be noticed—and driven back with sticks and stones before we ever lay eyes on our little house."

So, during the daytime, the buddies hid in some deserted spot. And when dark came, and most of the human population was indoors, they resumed their journey, following the route recommended by Patchy Pete—south, then west, and again south.

Sinbad and The Duke paid strict attention to the traffic and had no accident. Their only real problem was hunger. Never once did they find a handout in this land, which indeed seemed to be catless. And at night, when they came out of hiding, they had no opportunity for stealing, because every food shop was closed. The buddies had to live on mean pickings from streets and garbage cans. They had to quench their thirst with water left by the April showers in gutters or other hollow places.

Hopes of finding the little house kept up the spirit of the young tramps. Hope was strengthened by the increasing pleasantness of the surroundings, where the buildings became smaller and smaller and there were more gardens and sheds—but as yet no shacks.

It was on the fourth night of the journey that Sinbad and The Duke entered the oldest part of Little Old New York. That same night, before they had gone very far, the heaviest shower of April broke upon them and almost washed them from the sidewalk. They crawled through a railing and entered a garden that was crammed with bushes. But the small young leaves did not offer much protection from the rain.

The buddies peered about them with their see-through-the-darkness eyes and saw that deep within this tangled garden stood a

shack. No paths led to it. Whatever paths might formerly have existed were now over-run with bushes. The buddies squeezed their way through the bushes and came to a little old wooden shack, whose door was partly open.

They stepped inside. The roof did not leak. Dust covered the floor. But who were Sinbad and The Duke, to mind a bit of dust when the floor space was just the right size for boxing? A small sofa stood against one wall. The sofa was tattered, but it would be comfortable for sleeping.

A few toys lay in one corner of the room, as if waiting for their child owners to return and gather them up. Sinbad and The Duke sniffed the toys for signs of dangers. But the toys did not move, and the dust that rested thick on them buried the scent of their owners' hands. Those children must have long ago forgotten their playthings and this old playhouse. Anyway, no human, not even a child, could now push a way through the tangled garden. Here, in this shack, two cats would be safe.

"The house of our own," murmured the buddies. And their spirits soared.

Sinbad raised a big front paw and drove a hard right hook to The Duke's jaw. The Duke raised a big front paw and delivered a similar hard hook to Sinbad's jaw. And the buddies jabbed, punched, and pummeled each other across the dusty floor until they had given full expression to their joy.

Then they jumped up on the very old sofa and curled themselves close to one another. And while the rain beat down on the watertight roof, the raggedy young tramps fell alseep in the house of their own.

26

Early next morning, Sinbad and The Duke awoke to see the sunshine already streaming through the small window that was high up near the roof of their little house. The sunshine played on the walls and on the dusty floor.

"Niftiest little house that ever was," thought the young tramps.

They jumped down from their sofa and began to box. But they couldn't box for long, because they were weak from hunger. A day and a night had passed since they'd eaten anything. Those last mouthfuls had been the poorest sort of pickings.

Now that Sinbad and The Duke had found their house, they were ready to go forth in broad daylight and try their luck at robbing a food shop. If they were noticed, and if sticks and stones were thrown at them, they could fly back to their house—their safe retreat from humans. "But let's steer clear of humans, when we can," said Sinbad and The Duke.

The buddies squeezed through the tangled garden to the railing that protected it from the sidewalk. There they found a lookout, where they were concealed by the bushes, yet able to enjoy a good view of the street.

Children were thumping past the garden on their way to school. Children aroused a special terror in Sinbad, because once a boy had trapped him and tied a string and tin can on the end of his spiky tail. But these schoolchildren were soon out of sight, and only a few grownups dotted the sidewalks.

"Time for robbing," said the buddies.

They left their garden lookout for the sidewalk, and crept forward close to buildings, which they felt protected them from human sight. Two blocks from home they found a little fish shop that had an easy-to-push-open door.

The robbers entered the shop so cleverly that neither the swing of the door nor the tread of their paws made the slightest sound. The shopkeeper, who stood behind the counter, seemed quite unaware of what

was about to happen. He went on talking with his only customer, a woman who stood in front of the counter.

The robbers tiptoed to the counter and rose on their hind legs. Then each robber raised a big front paw, caught a hunk of fish, brought it down, clutched it in his mouth, and escaped to the sidewalk. They met at the curb and ate their loot in safety, beneath a parked car. The fish was raw and icy, but it seemed a real feast and would last them until next morning.

So they scurried home, apparently unnoticed, to the tangled garden. There they drank some water which last night's April shower had left in an empty tin can that an untidy human had thrown from the street into the garden. Then they boxed in their little house, and took a noontime nap, and in the afternoon they boxed again.

When night came and most humans were abed, Sinbad and The Duke sallied forth beneath the starry sky to learn more about their neighborhood. They strolled through quiet streets where few cars passed and no car honked a horn. They paused and sniffed the pleasant-smelling bricks of the little old houses in which the humans lived. They lingered to enjoy the fragrance that arose from the grass and other greenery of gardens.

The neighborhood seemed to have been made for cats. But Sinbad and The Duke could whiff no other paw prints on the sidewalk. They heard no mews or wails or songs behind a garden fence. They saw no cat-face at a window, peering down to view what might be happening in the streets.

"That old story must be true," thought the buddies. They meant, of course, the legend which Patchy Pete had told them about all cats having been driven away long ago because some had done mischief.

The absence of cats did not bother Sinbad and The Duke. The two buddies did not seek the companionship of others of their kind. Indeed, the buddies felt they would never wish for anyone except themselves.

That night, when they returned home from their stroll, they said, "Niftiest little neighborhood that ever was." And they hoped their luck would let them live forever in this pleasant part of Little Old New York.

Alas! Their luck at robbing food shops did not last.

One morning, while they were at the counter of the fish shop, the shopkeeper caught sight of them. He did not kick them out. He let them escape with their loot. But next morning, when they pushed his door, a bell at the top of it tinkled, warned him of their arrival, and made them withdraw.

After that Sinbad and The Duke robbed other fish shops and some meat shops. But within a couple of weeks all the little food shops in the neighborhood were protected by those tinkling bells, which made it well-nigh impossible for a cat to enter and steal.

"Let's try our luck at catching birds," said the buddies.

Alas! They had no luck at all with the birds. This seemed strange, be-cause these pigeons and sparrows that pattered about on the sidewalk had probably never seen  a cat. Perhaps the cats who lived here in olden times had been such ferocious hunters that the memory of their doings had been handed down from generation to generation of birds. Be that as it may, these present-day birds were wise to the ambitions of Sinbad and The Duke. The buddies caught never a mouthful of bird.

"So it's pickings for us," sighed the bud-dies.

Alas! Their luck with pickings was the worst they'd ever encountered. Night after night they sallied forth from their little house, poked about in gutters and garbage cans, and found barely enough to keep them-selves alive.

Milk, of course, was a thing of the past. Then water became a problem. No more water pools were left by April showers. April had been taken over by the bright, clear month of May, which shed no rain. Sinbad and The Duke eventually discovered a leaky pipe in the side of a building. From the pipe came drops of rusty water that saved them from dying of thirst. But the two cats were always hungry.

One afternoon, while they sat at the door-way of their home, Sinbad said to The Duke, "Let's go back to The Tramps' Last Stop for one good meal."

The Duke hesitated and then replied, "I'd hate to leave our little house even for a few nights."

Sinbad said, "We would come back to it."

The Duke said, "But what about the neighborhood? I have a funny feeling we'd be turning our backs on our own neighbor-hood."

Sinbad demanded, "What's so nifty about a neighborhood that doesn't give us any handouts? Don't argue with me, Duke. Don't remind me that Patchy Pete warned us not to expect any handouts in this part of town. And don't tell me we should make the best of things. I'm hungry. You're hungry. And people in this neighborhood know we're here and hungry. Didn't people see us when we robbed the food shops? Didn't people see us when we chased the birds? But not one of those humans took pity on us. Not one of them ever gave us a handout."

The Duke then said, "Maybe those people couldn't track us down to where we live."

"Phooey," retorted Sinbad. "A handout could be left in any quiet spot, and we would find it."

The Duke said, "Maybe by now those people think we've moved away."

Sinbad argued, "Others, too, have seen us. And just last night, when we were near that streetlamp and overturned that garbage can to get at pickings, people heard the bang-

bang of the can. And before we scrammed, lots of people stuck their old heads out of windows and someone cried, 'Look! There they are, those cats!' "

The Duke sighed and said, "And here we are, hungrier than ever. Sinbad, you never were a beauty, and now your ribs are almost poking through your skin. Oh, Sinbad, my poor Sinbad! I'm ready to trek north with you to The Tramps' Last Stop for one good bite of chicken à la king."

But now it was Sinbad's turn to hesitate. He did so and then said, "Wait! I've been thinking about last night when we upset the garbage can, and people shouted at us, but no one threw sticks or stones. No one in this neighborhood has ever thrown a stick or stone at us. And even Patchy Pete, who was here last fall, warned us about sticks and stones. Maybe this neighborhood has changed since Patchy Pete was here, or maybe it's changing now."

Indeed, at that moment, both the buddies felt that something new and strange might be hovering in their air. They sniffed the air for a whiff of food. Alas! They sniffed in vain. But they agreed to stay a while longer in the neighborhood and give it one more chance to show a little kindness in regard to handouts.

Now, that very evening, as the buddies left their tangled garden for a pickings expedition, their noses twitched.

"Liver!" murmured Sinbad.

"Fresh liver!" murmured The Duke.

"Seeing's believing," said Sinbad.

"Step this way," said The Duke.

They stepped together to a crumbling, old brick building where there was a deserted barbershop. The shop had a glass window that was surrounded by a wooden framework. The bottom of the framework had long ago been smashed in such a manner that it formed an open space. Across a part of this open space, a human had newly tacked a sheet of cardboard that served as a protective screen. And behind this screen, Sinbad and The Duke found a supper for two. It consisted of a plate heaped with fresh, sliced liver. There was also a bowl of sweet milk, as well as another bowl of clear, fresh water.

"Somebody likes us!" cried the buddies. And without another word, they fell to their supper which, thanks to the cardboard screen, they could eat in privacy and peace.

After they had licked the plate clean, the buddies lingered in the nook. They were curious about the human who had given them this splendid handout. So they sniffed the edges of the plate and of the bowls and of the cardboard screen. Along the edges were fingerprints which indicated that the human was a man. The newness of the prints also indicated that he had come to the nook just before the evening hour.

"And then he went away and let us eat by ourselves," said Sinbad.

"And in such a nifty supper nook," said The Duke.

"And so close to home," said Sinbad.

The Duke suggested, "Maybe he spotted us last night when we upset the garbage can, and maybe he saw which way we ran."

And both cats wondered, "Does he know we've settled in this neighborhood? Will he come again?"

Bright and early next morning, the buddies stationed themselves at their garden lookout. All day long they watched their street for the sight of the man who had given them their last night's supper. But they saw no one who seemed to be their man.

Then, just before the evening hour, when most humans were indoors at their supper tables, the buddies saw a tall, slender, easy-walking man come around a far corner of

the block. This was someone whom they'd never seen.

"He's carrying a basket," said Sinbad.

"He's going to our supper nook," said The Duke.

"He's pulling back the screen," said Sinbad.

"He's taking things from his basket," said
The Duke.

"Our man," declared the buddies in their
single voice. And they watched their man
replace the screen, walk away, and disap-
pear around his corner. Whereupon they ran
to the supper nook and cried, "Wow!"

For they found that last evening's soiled
crockery had been removed, and in its place,
on clean crockery, there was a brand new
supper. It consisted of a plate of fish—not
raw and icy, but boneless, cooked, and fluffy
—and a bowl of sweet milk and another bowl
of fresh water.

"Wow!" became the buddies' evening cry
of joy, because evening after evening their
man appeared at the same hour and re-
stocked their supper nook. Sometimes it was
chopped beef. Sometimes it was those crispy
little balls that came from boxes and were
called "Kittens' Munchies." Sometimes it was

good canned cat food that might be accompanied by scraps of roast chicken. All these and other delicacies took turns in appearing on the supper plate. And each meal was hearty enough to last the buddies until next evening.

A Strange Sight
in Another Garden

Sinbad and The Duke of course felt grateful toward the man who fed them. But they never tried to thank him. Never, in fact, did they go near him. They only watched him from their garden lookout.

The man, for his part, never tried to find them. All he did was to come quietly to their supper nook at the close of every day and lay out their meal and then walk away, as if he wished no thanks.

One day this man, whom Sinbad and The

Duke now called the master of the supper nook, stayed longer than usual at the nook. The buddies, from their garden lookout, could see that he was busying himself with the screen, which had enabled them to eat in privacy.

After he left, they hurried to the nook and found that he had replaced the old, flimsy, cardboard screen with a new, strong, wooden one. He had hinged its top firmly to the framework of the nook so that he could lift up the screen and thus easily spread out the supper. But the cats, for their convenience in getting at the supper, could slip

through a hole—a cat-size doorway—that had been cut into the bottom of the screen.

"Nifty screen," said Sinbad.

"Wind can't blow it away," said The Duke.

"Looks like the master of our supper nook is going to go on feeding us," said Sinbad.

"Looks like forever," said The Duke.

"Forever! Wow!" they cried joyfully. And they fell to eating their excellent supper. But after supper, while they lingered in the nook, their joy gave way to woe.

"Listen," said Sinbad. And he spoke heavily, as if he'd have to drag each word from the bottom of his paws.

"I'm listening," replied The Duke, in the dull voice of one who doesn't wish to hear what's going to be said.

Sinbad muttered, "We'll have to thank the master of this supper nook."

"Why?" demanded The Duke.

"Because," replied Sinbad, "we can't go on eating here forever unless we thank the man who feeds us."

"But Sinbad, we've never thanked a human for a handout. And besides, our man doesn't seem to want our thanks. He seems to understand why tramps like us should steer clear of humans. Oh, he's kind himself, and wouldn't ever hurt us. But all his world, the human world, is filled with traps for tramps. Don't you remember the boy who tied a tin can on the end of your tail? Believe me, my dear Sinbad, much worse than that can happen to tramps who go too close to humans."

"My dear Duke, you're right. Let's skip the thanks," said Sinbad.

The Duke, however, took up the other side of argument, saying, "But our man comes here day after day, rain or shine, to feed us."

"My dear Duke, as you yourself have already so beautifully put it, we've never thanked a human for a handout. Why do it now?"

"Because," replied The Duke, "in the old days we were always on the move, from place to place. But now we've settled in this neighborhood. We really ought—somehow, sometime—to thank the man who runs our supper nook. It's what Patchy Pete would call a neighborhood obligation."

"A neighborhood obligation," murmured Sinbad. "Hmmmmm. I do remember Patchy Pete said little duties would arise. OK, Duke, we might as well go through with this one. But let's be cautious with it. Let it be our last."

So there, in the supper nook, the young tramps thought up what seemed to them a safe and simple plan to thank the man who fed them. They'd go late some night to the man's house, when he would probably be abed, and they'd thank the outside of his house.

"Just the outside of his house, no more than that," said Sinbad.

"And afterward we'll scoot home and box," said The Duke.

Neither of the buddies was troubled by

the fact that their man might never know they'd come. They were thinking only that the little thank-you trip would ease their hearts.

"When shall we go?" asked Sinbad.

"Tonight, and get our obligation over with," replied The Duke.

Sinbad agreed to this, and the buddies remained in the supper nook until what seemed to them a safe, quiet time of night. Then each of them passed a wet paw over

his face. This was nearly all the washing that they ever did, and they did not do it often. They did it now out of respect for the man whom they were going to thank.

Washing their faces at this time made the raggedy young tramps feel that they were preparing for a tremendous journey. Their thoughts were sober as they left the supper nook and lowered their noses to the sidewalk to pick up the scent of the man's footprints.

His trail led the buddies west for one block, and then south along a street which they had seldom visited because it had no food shops and its opportunities for pickings were slim. But the buddies had ventured here on that famous night not so long ago when they upset the garbage can and brought people to the windows, crying, "There they are, those cats!"

Well, here they were, those very cats, and presently they reached that very garbage can. But they did not need to stop now and investigate it. Their starvation period was over, and they were on their way to thank the man who fed them.

His trail soon brought them to a row of little brick houses that stood shoulder to shoulder. All these houses had darkened windows and looked much alike, except for one house that was covered with vines. The trail ended at the closed door of this vine-covered house.

"Here's where he lives," said Sinbad.

"Here's where he's sleeping," said The Duke.

They stepped back toward the edge of the sidewalk and, gazing at the front of their man's house, each cat waved a paw of thanks. The hearts of both cats then felt eased of a burden—but not all of the burden.

Sinbad said, "We haven't thanked him quite enough."

The Duke agreed and said, "Let's thank the back of his house."

No sooner said than off they set. But they had to travel nearly all around the block before they found a passage to the back of the vine-covered house. This was because on all four sides of the block were these rows of little houses, standing body to body, with no passage between them, except on the block's fourth side. Here was an opening— a short, narrow alley that led to a tall, board fence.

Sinbad and The Duke went down the alley, jumped to the top of the fence, and saw a garden. It was not a little, tangled, weedy garden like their own. This was the most spacious, well-kept garden they had ever seen. The long, smooth carpet of fresh-cut grass was enlivened with a few graceful bushes. And at the far end, near a corner, stood a tall tree, whose branches were covered with leaves that shimmered in the moonlight.

"Just you and me," thought the young tramps. And they felt a wave of awe rise in them from their belief that they were the only cats in a catless land—the sole cats of nowadays to view this wonderful garden.

The buddies then turned their attention to the purpose of their visit. They saw that all around the garden, except for the board fence on which they stood, were the backs of the little houses, which looked very much the same, except the one that was covered with vines. All, except the vine-covered one, which was in the middle of a side row, had darkened windows. This house had an upstairs window that was lighted. No one, however, could be seen at the window.

"Our man's house, and he's probably gone to sleep with his light on," murmured Sinbad.

"We're safe," murmured The Duke.

The top of the fence was too narrow for

them to stand on, balance themselves, and at the same time wave a paw. So they jumped down into the garden and there, on firm ground by the fence, they gazed at the back of their man's house and waved the paw of thanks. Both cats now felt free and easy. They had no further obligation and could go home.

But just as they were about to jump the fence, they were halted by the cry of a cat:

Trip-a-la, trip-a-lee!

It was not a hunger cry. This was the happy call to something, and it was sung by the voice of a young she-cat.

Great was the buddies' astonishment at the sound of a cat in the land that was supposed to be catless. They looked toward where the cry had come from—toward the far end of the garden, where there was the leafy tree. Near that tree, at the low, open window of one of the little houses, stood a white cat.

The astonishment of Sinbad and The Duke gave way to curiosity. They crouched by the fence, stretched forth their necks, and stared.

The white cat jumped to the ground. She was a slim, graceful creature.

Trip-a-la, trip-a-lee!

she sang once more. Then she sped across the grass, singing:

Trip-a-la, trip-a-lee,
We meet at the tree!

When she reached the tree, she climbed its trunk, disappeared among the leafage, and ceased her song.

Whereupon, from the low window of a different house at the same far end of the garden, crawled a small, yellowish cat, who walked gravely to the tree and sat down beneath it. Then, from the low window of a house midway along the garden, came a fluffy, silvery cat who stepped lightly to the tree and sat down near the yellowish one. And now, from a low window midway on the opposite side of the garden, emerged another white cat. He was a big, fat fellow, who marched slowly and seated himself importantly between the yellowish and silvery arrivals.

The three cats beneath the tree remained quietly seated, as if they were engaged in earnest conversation.

"Pet cats out for a gab," thought Sinbad and The Duke. "But why does their pal, the one who did the singing, stay in the tree?"

The young tramps cupped their ears. However, the words of what was being said at the tree did not travel as far as the fence.

At last the three cats beneath the tree stood up, and the slim white one—the singer —climbed down the trunk and joined them, and the meeting broke up.

The slim white one and the yellowish one walked separately to the far end of the garden and disappeared through the open windows of their houses. The other two cats— the fat white one and the fluffy silvery one— walked together as far as the middle of the garden, where they parted. Each of these two now proceeded to his or her own side of the garden. But they lingered, each at his or her own window.

The fluffy silvery one called out across the garden to the fat white one, "Until tomorrow night, Mr. President."

The fat white one, who had been addressed as "Mr. President," called back to the fluffy, silvery one, "Yes, Madame Butterfly, our Cat Club shall meet again tomorrow night, at the same hour, at this same spot, beneath the maple tree."

"We'll be there, too," murmured Sinbad and The Duke.

A Closer View
of the Cat Club

Curiosity—and curiosity alone—made Sinbad and The Duke wish to go back next evening to the big garden. They wanted to know what had brought those four pets into a neighborhood that was thought to be catless. How long had those four pets been living here? And what was this club of theirs which held nightly meetings at the maple tree?

Sinbad and The Duke did not wish to get

mixed up in the affairs of those pet cats. A pet cat was a cat who had a home in the human world and as a consequence he had household obligations. For example, a pet cat might go outdoors from time to time, but sooner or later a human voice would call, "Come, puss, come here, come home."

"What a narrow life a pet cat leads," thought Sinbad and The Duke.

It is true that Sinbad and The Duke themselves had once been pets—happy, grateful pets. But that time seemed long ago. Now they were tramps, and neither the house of their own nor the supper nook had changed their trampish love of the free and easy life.

The free and easy life, for these young tramps, meant the right to get up when they pleased and to go to bed when they pleased, and during the rest of the time to roam wherever they pleased or to do whatever else they pleased to please their own sweet selves. Small wonder that Sinbad and The Duke did not wish to tangle in the affairs of any pet cats.

"But those four who live by that big garden are living in this neighborhood," said Sinbad.

"And it's our own neighborhood, and we should spend a little time in finding out a thing or two about the Cat Club," said The Duke.

That they might satisfy their curiosity, the young tramps thought up what seemed to them another of their safe and simple plans. When night fell, they'd go over to that garden, hide in the topmost leafage of the maple tree and there, unseen, they'd watch and listen to what happened round about them.

The plan required no preparation—not even the washing of a face. So, after a fine supper, Sinbad and The Duke merely waited for the coming of dark. Then they scurried over to the big garden, jumped its tall board fence, dashed to the maple tree, climbed

the trunk, and settled themselves on a bough among the leafage at the treetop.

"Guess no one saw us coming," murmured Sinbad.

"Guess no one can ever see us here," murmured The Duke.

They were indeed well hidden in the leafy treetop. But they enjoyed a good view of the ground below and of the moonlit garden and of the rows of little houses that surrounded it. How tiny those houses seemed compared to the high-rise buildings which loomed in the far distance and thrust their towers up to the starry sky. And now the lights in the little houses were going out.

"People's bedtime," thought the tramps.

One light, and only one, remained. It was the light at the upstairs window of the vine-covered house—the house of the master of the supper nook. The tramps wondered if their kind friend knew that four pet cats from these very houses would soon hold a club meeting at the maple tree.

The first to come was the slim white one. She sped gracefully across the garden, singing her song:

> *Trip-a-la, trip-a-lee,*
> *We meet at the tree!*

But when she reached the foot of the tree, she ceased her song and sniffed the air, as if she sniffed the smell of strangers.

"Detected," thought the tramps. "We should've washed before coming. But never mind, we can't be caught. We can fight off any cat who climbs up here to nab us. And we won't get down for anyone."

The slim white cat sniffed the air again. She was somewhat older than the visitors, but she was still a young thing, and she acted

now as if she'd better mind her own affairs. So she climbed the tree to its lowest bough and lay down there. Then she stretched her right front paw along the bough, as if in readiness for the business that really concerned her.

The next to come was the small yellow cat. He was old and wizened and wore red whiskers. When he reached the meeting ground he too sniffed the air suspiciously. But he said nothing and sat down quietly,

as if lost in his own deep thoughts.

The two other cats were on their way. The fat white one, known as Mr. President, and the fluffy silvery Madame Butterfly were

walking side by side. Mr. President was middle-aged. Madame Butterfly might have been almost as old as Mr. President, but she was lively and beautiful.

When they arrived at the meeting ground, Madame Butterfly said in a gay, rippling voice, "Mr. President, I smell a trampy smell."

"My dear Madame Butterfly," replied Mr. President in a solemn, pompous voice—and he cast a sharp glance at the treetop—"I, too, smell a trampy smell. But first things come first. Let us begin our meeting, discuss our business, and afterward I shall deal with the trampy smell."

"He'll never lay a paw on us," thought the young tramps in the treetop. And then and there they hated Mr. President. They sent him boiling glances as he seated himself

on the ground at the foot of the tree, between Madame Butterfly and the wizened yellow one.

"The meeting will come to order," announced Mr. President.

The slim white cat who lay on the low bough opened the claws of her right paw and scratched something into the bark.

Then Mr. President said, "This is the third meeting of the Cat Club. Our plans thus far have gone well. We have a President, who is myself. We have a Secretary, Miss Concertina, who scratches the records of our meetings."

Scratch! Scratch! went the claws of the slim white cat as she dug them vigorously into the bark of her low bough.

And the President continued, saying, "We

also have two regular members, the gracious Madame Butterfly and Solomon the Wise Cat."

"Present," squeaked the small yellow wizened fellow in an absent-minded voice.

"Yes, Solomon," said the President in a smooth, patient voice, "we know that you are present. We shall listen now to anything that you may have discovered about the gentleman who owns this garden. We ourselves know little more than what we have seen. We've seen him come out of his house in the daylight hours and dig and plant in all four corners of the garden—and then go back into his house—the vine-covered house."

The tramps in the treetop thought, "So the master of this garden is the master of our supper nook." And they perked their ears to catch all that Solomon might say about the gentleman.

"His heart is large," said Solomon.

"Yes," said the President, "that we know,

because he lets our Club use his garden. But what else, Solomon, have you found out from your books of knowledge or from other sources?"

Said Solomon, "Late this afternoon I managed to slip, unnoticed, into the gentleman's house. He was leaving it, carrying a basket of food."

"Our supper," thought the tramps.

Solomon continued, saying, "In his absence I poked about his house."

"Does he have any cats?" asked the President.

"No cats, Mr. President, and nobody else lives with him. But he's the sort of man who sooner or later will take in a cat. Some little cat, maybe, who needs a home."

"Won't be us," thought the tramps. "Can't

ever be us because there's two of us and we're no kittens and we've a house of our own. We're safe." But they were more curious than ever about this kindly man who fed them.

Solomon was saying, "Our gentleman at present is busy getting settled in his vine-covered house."

"Ah," said the President, "he's like the masters and mistresses with whom we came. He's a new arrival at this garden. Why is it that we all moved here at the same time?"

"Not quite the same time, Mr. President," replied Solomon. "Our gentleman, the master of this garden, arrived first. Then he spread the news that cats might use his garden. And that, I guess, is why our owners brought us into this land which used to be catless. Rest assured, Mr. President, that with such a gentleman in our midst, cats will be welcome not only in this garden but throughout the neighborhood."

"Ah, Solomon," said the President. "The

report which you are giving us strengthens my hopes about our Club's future activities."

The tramps in the treetop wished the President would stop interrupting Solomon. They felt the President made interruptions just to hear the sound of his own voice.

But the wizened old yellow wise cat did not seem to mind the presidential interruptions. He went on to say, "As to the gentleman in question, he has lots of furnishings and bright cloths and strange shells. That's why it's taking him so long to get settled."

"What sort of gentleman do you think he is?" asked the President.

"An old sea captain who has but recently retired from the sea," replied Solomon.

"Why do you think so?" asked the President.

"Because," replied Solomon, "his belongings—those shells and other things—have a salty smell which, according to my books of knowledge, is the smell of the sea."

"Solomon, why should an old sea captain

be so fond of a garden?" asked the President.

Said Solomon, "Old sea captains grow weary of all the rolling water in the world. That's why, in the end, they like the feel of grass and solid earth beneath their feet."

"But why, Solomon," said the President, "why should an old sea captain like ours show a special understanding of cats? Our captain, for example, manages to make our Club feel welcome in his garden. But he is careful never to come near us, nor in any other way does he disturb our activities."

Solomon replied, "Almost every ship carries her own cat, not only to catch rats but to keep the captain and the sailors company on those long and lonely voyages at sea. An old sea captain, such as ours, who has spent his life on ships, has had plenty of time in which to study the nature of cats. He has learned that cats, however much they may love humans, need moments of privacy in which to pursue their own thoughts."

"And activities," added the President, who

seemed unable to resist this opportunity of putting in his own two words. He sounded also as if he'd like to say more.

But Solomon exclaimed, "Look! There's our captain. He's standing at the lighted window of his vine-covered house."

The whole Club turned their heads and gazed at the shadowy figure of the captain. So did Sinbad and The Duke.

"The master of our garden," announced the President.

"The master of our supper nook," thought the tramps.

The President said, "Let the Cat Club raise a cry of thanks to the gentleman who permits us to use his garden."

The Club raised a cry of thanks. The old sea captain replied by waving a friendly hand. Then he disappeared from his window and left the Club to its own doings.

The brief appearance of the captain had cast a pleasant spell upon the garden. The spell was broken now by a cough from the President. It was a cough that called attention to himself and to what he was preparing to say.

The young tramps in the treetop thought, "Old Windbag's getting up his steam."

And they heard Old Windbag say, "Solomon's excellent report and the gracious appearance of our captain makes me confident that our Club will be able to fulfill its purpose. Let me again remind the Club of this purpose. Our purpose, which has been set down in our Rules and Obligations—"

"Rules and Obligations," thought the tramps. "Bet Old Windbag made them up himself."

"Our purpose," continued Old Windbag, "the purpose of our Club is to serve neighborhood cats. Yes, to serve all neighborhood cats as a center of worthwhile activities."

"Worthwhile activities! What garbage!" thought the tramps. And they felt they'd listened to all they cared to hear about Old Windbag's Cat Club. But a rippling voice caught their attention. It was the voice of the beautiful Madame Butterfly.

"Mr. President," said she, "worthwhile activities are important. So are fun and frolic."

"My dear Madame Butterfly," replied Old Windbag, "we shall discuss fun and frolic when the time comes. Meanwhile let us deal with tonight's more urgent business."

Old Windbag lifted his fat face toward the treetop and called, "Will our visitors please come down?"

The young tramps did not answer. They did not budge.

Face to Face
with the President

Then, for the second time, Old Windbag called, "Will our visitors in the treetop please come down?"

Again, Sinbad and The Duke did not answer. Nor did they budge.

"Will our visitors please come down?" he called once more.

This time his voice surprised them. It was a presidential voice, that had to be obeyed. So they climbed slowly down the tree and stood behind it.

"Will our visitors please step forward?" said the President. They walked around to the meeting ground.

"Closer," he said, motioning with his paw to a spot in front of him.

They walked to the spot and stood face to face with the President of the Cat Club. His smooth whiteness made them feel raggedy and dirty. Madame Butterfly gave them a smile of encouragement. The smile did not help. They thought only of the President and hated him completely.

The President stared at them as if he'd never seen such wild-looking cats. But in a moment he gathered himself together and in a voice that he tried to make sound very pleasant, asked them, "What are your names?"

"Sinbad and The Duke," they answered, using their single voice so that the President could not tell which one of them was which. He did not seem to mind, but acted as if he'd save that little matter for a later date.

"Tell me, Sinbad and The Duke," he continued, "do you live in this neighborhood?"

They nodded.

"Whereabouts?" he asked.

"Beyond the fence," they answered. And then, because they didn't wish to have the President's fat paw meddling with their free and easy life, they added, "Our house doesn't have a number."

The President said, "My young friends, house numbers are not important. What does matter is that you live in the neighborhood and have shown an interest in this Cat Club. Our Club, as you may have heard, serves as a center of worthwhile activities for neighborhood cats."

"Haw! Haw!" laughed the buddies.

The President paid no attention to their insolence. He went on to say, "It is not difficult for a cat to become a member of the Club. We have very simple Rules and Obligations."

At those words, "Rules and Obligations," the buddies gave another, louder "haw! haw!" which the President brushed from the air with his fat paw.

Said he, "The principal Rule is that a member should possess some special talent or knowledge. The principal Obligation is that a member should be willing at all times to contribute his special talent or knowledge for the benefit of the other members. Now let me ask you, Sinbad and The Duke, are you interested in joining our Cat Club?"

"No!" they cried.

The President set his jaw, like a mighty cat who would not take "no" for an answer. Then he said in a sweet, coaxing voice, "Perhaps I have made the Cat Club sound too severe. Let me add that we shall have nights of fun and frolic. I am sure, Sinbad and The Duke, that you could do something to entertain the membership—just some little thing, like singing a song or telling a joke."

Here was the buddies' chance. Here was their opportunity to show Old Windbag the stuff of which they were made. Sinbad drove a hard right hook to The Duke's jaw. The Duke delivered a similar hard hook to Sinbad's jaw. And then, casting aside all rules for boxing, they punched and pummeled one another and began to roll.

They rolled to the left, and without meaning to, they knocked into Solomon. They rolled to the right, and without meaning to, they bumped into Madame Butterfly. Next, they rolled straight ahead, and this time, after taking good aim, they lunged smack into Old Windbag.

"Halt!" he cried.

They halted and grinned.

"Go back to your places," he commanded.

They did as they were told. Solomon gazed quietly at the sky, and Madame Butterfly gave them a smile of forgiveness. Old Windbag steadied himself, as though making ready for another effort to pull the young tramps into his Club.

"Sinbad and The Duke," he began in his smooth voice, "your boxing is clever, but for Club purposes it is too rough."

"We like to box rough," they retorted.

He said, "But if you toned your boxing down into something daintier, it would be suitable for us. And then you could join the Club and entertain us with exhibition matches on our nights of fun and frolic."

"We like to box rough," they insisted.

"Think it over," he urged.

"Go twiddle your whiskers," they shouted.

The buddies then felt it was high time for them to leave. But the President fixed them to the spot with his beady eyes.

"My young friends," said he, in his very smoothest voice, "let me know if you ever change your minds about wishing to join the Cat Club."

He paused long enough to let those words sink in. And then he said, "Visitors, of course, are always welcome. But they must wash themselves before coming."

82

There was another pause, after which he said, "You may leave now, if you wish."

Sinbad and The Duke fled from the meeting ground and hurried home. They hurried because they had an uneasy feeling that the President was pursuing them and would try again to rope them into his Cat Club. They did not feel safe until they were well inside the little house of their own, where they snorted, "That Old Windbag."

"And his worthwhile activities," jeered Sinbad.

"Or a little song or a little joke, or else some dainty boxing that'll entertain the other members," jeered The Duke.

"Visitors, of course, are always welcome," snickered Sinbad.

"But they must wash themselves before coming," snickered The Duke.

Then, through the minds of these tramps flashed the silvery face of Madame Butterfly.

"Madame Butterfly smiled at us," murmured Sinbad.

"She's quite a dame," murmured The Duke.

"But the President's the boss," said Sinbad.

"He'd like to trap us with his Rules and Obligations," said The Duke.

"Let him twiddle his whiskers," declared the buddies in their single voice.

Little Mac

The master of the supper nook continued to provide Sinbad and The Duke with a delicious supper every night, and they were always grateful. But they avoided going near him, or his house, or his garden, which was the meeting place for the Cat Club.

Now and then the young tramps thought wistfully of the two smiles that Madame Butterfly had given them. But those smiles did not wipe out the memory of the Club's terrible President. The buddies rejoiced that they had escaped his clutches and his Rules and Obligations.

"The free and easy life for us," they thought. And they felt happy that they could now enjoy this kind of life. For they had their own house, and a beautifully run supper nook, and nothing to do but to live as they pleased—to please themselves.

So they spent oodles of time in boxing at home. However, even future champs can grow tired of boxing by themselves. It soon became a lonely sport for Sinbad and The Duke, and they began to wish for an audience. They wanted to hear the voices of other cats, such as the rippling voice of Madame Butterfly, shouting, "Bravo, Sinbad! Bravo, Duke!" Or else to hear the voice of some wise critic, like the old tramp, Patchy Pete, saying, "You must practice your skips and shuffles."

One night, while the buddies were out on an idle stroll, they saw a cat sitting in the distance, at the top of the high staircase of a house near a streetlamp.

"A new arrival in the neighborhood," they thought.

The stranger called out to them, "Hi!"

His voice was that of a pet cat. But it sounded so young and pleasant that Sinbad and The Duke, who had nothing else to do, walked toward him. When they reached the foot of the staircase and looked up at him, they liked what they saw. He was much younger than they, and clean and soft. His light grey fur was prettily marked with very regular stripes of a darker grey. His face had a loving, trustful expression.

"Hi, little fella, do you live here?" they asked him in a friendly voice.

"Yes, my master and I moved into this house a couple of days ago. We have the first-floor apartment, right here by this open window," replied the youngster.

"What's your name?" they asked.

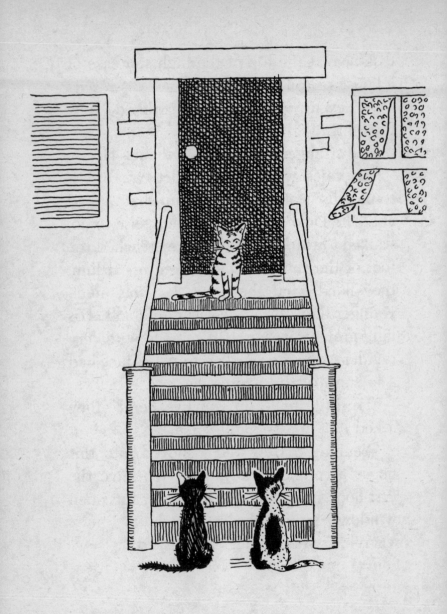

"Macaroni," he replied. "What's yours?"

"Sinbad and The Duke," they answered.

"Which is which?" asked Macaroni.

"I'm Sinbad," replied the one with the yellow ear.

"I'm the other fella," said The Duke.

"Do you live in the neighborhood?" asked Macaroni.

"Yes, Little Mac, we have a house of our own not far from here," replied the buddies in their single voice.

"I'm glad you live nearby," he said. "I'm glad because I'm lonesome."

"Does your master neglect you?" they asked in a sympathetic tone.

"No, not really," answered Little Mac. "My master feeds me well, and last winter he spent lots of time with me and taught me to dance. But he's a young man, and now that spring is here, he leaves home right after supper and goes out to dance somewhere himself. I'm alone for hours and hours, and that's why I'm lonesome in the night. May I dance for you?"

The buddies did not expect much entertainment from so young a cat. However, they could understand why he wanted an audience, because they had lately had a lonely time in boxing by themselves, with no one to appreciate what they could do. So they said to him, "OK. Wiggle away."

"I'll dance the Patpaw Polka," he announced.

Little Mac rose on his hind legs and capered back and forth across the stoop so prettily that Sinbad and The Duke were impressed. They felt proud of him, as though he were a talented younger brother.

"Nifty dancing, Little Mac," they told him when the Patpaw Polka came to an end.

"I'm learning the Pitty-pat Waltz. It's fancier than the polka and needs lots of practice," he said.

"Well, Little Mac, practicing at night should keep you busy while your master's away," said Sinbad and The Duke.

"But I can't practice all the time," sighed Little Mac. "And what I really want to do is to dance for other cats. I want them to enjoy my dancing. May I dance for you again?"

Sinbad and The Duke thought to themselves: "The Cat Club is the place for him."

And then aloud they said, "Listen. Not far from here there's a center of activities for neighborhood cats. It's called the Cat Club. You ought to join it."

"Do you belong?" he asked.

"No, Little Mac," said they, "we have other things to do. But we'll tell you how to get there."

"Tell me now!" cried Little Mac excitedly. And he hurried down the staircase and joined the two tramps on the sidewalk.

The buddies noticed then that his paws were soft, as if he'd never walked on anything but floors and carpets.

"Little Mac," they said, "how much do you know about sidewalks and streets and cars and traffic lights?"

"Not much," he admitted. "This is the first time I've ever been on any sidewalk. But just the same, I'm going to the Cat Club— and going now."

Suddenly the buddies had an anxious feeling, just like that of older brothers worrying about the safety of a younger one.

"No, Little Mac," they said, "you shan't go now, all by yourself."

"Why?" he demanded.

"Because," said they, "you'd get chopped to pieces by the traffic."

But Little Mac said, "I'd rather be

chopped to pieces by the traffic than die of lonesomeness at home. And anyway, some night soon, when you're not here, I'll try to find the Cat Club on my own."

"You'll do nothing of the sort," they snapped.

"What'll I do?" he wailed.

"Give us time to think," said they.

Sinbad and The Duke thought to themselves and struggled with the same thoughts: "Are we obliged to take this youngster to the Cat Club? No, we aren't his parents . . . But he's a new cat in the neighborhood, our neighborhood. And he's lonesome and he'd like the Cat Club. What's the harm if we help him get there? Why, Old Windbag would laugh ha-ha to see us boxers turning up again . . . But what difference would a ha-ha from Old Windbag make to us? No diff, no diff at all . . . But, but, if Windbag ever laughs at Little Mac, oh, broken whiskers! it'll be another story."

Sinbad and The Duke began to wash. They washed not only their faces, but all the rest of their raggedy selves.

"What are you doing?" asked Little Mac.

"Brushing off the dust," said they.

"But why so late at night?" he asked.

"Because," said they, "we're going to take you to the Cat Club."

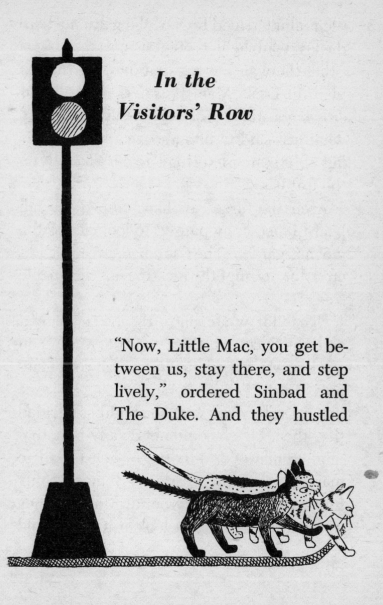

In the
Visitors' Row

"Now, Little Mac, you get between us, stay there, and step lively," ordered Sinbad and The Duke. And they hustled their young friend toward the garden where the Cat Club held its meetings.

On the way the two buddies tried to explain to Little Mac the safest methods for crossing a street. But he scarcely listened to what was said to him about cars and traffic lights. His mind seemed to be entirely on the Cat Club.

After the three cats had jumped the tall board fence, they paused to look across the moonlit garden. The Club had already gathered for its nightly meeting at the maple tree.

"That fat white one's the boss," Sinbad and The Duke explained to Little Mac. "You call him Mr. President, and watch your manners."

For Little Mac's sake, the buddies decided they themselves should not do anything that might ruffle Old Windbag. They began to march their youngster slowly, almost primly toward the meeting ground. Midway they paused to take a closer look at it. "Same old

Club, and not a whisker changed," they thought.

Indeed, Old Windbag was sitting at the foot of the maple tree. He seemed as fat and white and smooth as ever. On his left sat the fluffy, silvery, and lovely Madame Butterfly. On his right sat the yellow one, the wizened Solomon the Wise. And overhead, through the green leafage of the low bough, hung the slim, white tail of Secretary Concertina.

A discussion was being held. Sinbad and The Duke could not hear what it was about. It sounded unimportant. And besides, as they moved forward, all talking ceased. So they took Little Mac onto the meeting ground and right up before the President.

The President did not laugh at the return of Sinbad and The Duke. On the contrary, he seemed to note with serious approval that the two tramps had washed themselves and had brought along the sort of youngster who would cause no trouble.

Then the President said in a pleasant

voice, "Good evening, Sinbad and The Duke. Visitors, as you know, are always welcome. I have, in fact, reserved a special row for visitors."

He motioned with his fat paw to a place farther in front of him and just beyond the actual meeting ground.

"Listen, Mr. President," said Sinbad and The Duke. "Visitors' row is all right for us two buddies. But this young fella that's with us—our Little Mac—oughtn't to have to sit there. He's a dancer. Niftiest dancer that ever was."

"Ah," said the President, with a cordial nod to Little Mac.

"Mr. President," continued Sinbad and

The Duke, "we told Little Mac about your center of activities. He wants to join it. But he couldn't get here by himself. Doesn't know how to cross the streets alone. That's why we brought him here ourselves."

"Sinbad and The Duke," said the President, "it was kind of you to bring your young friend to the Cat Club. I thank you."

"The pleasure was ours," replied Sinbad and The Duke, using the grand expression that they had once heard from the lips of their old tramp friend, Patchy Pete.

Madame Butterfly gave the buddies a flashing smile. Then they stepped back and seated themselves in the visitors' row. Little Mac was left standing before the President.

"Little Mac, what is your real name?" asked the President in a friendly voice.

"Macaroni."

"Where do you live?"

"Mr. President, I can't tell you exactly where, because my master and I have just moved in. It's the house with the high staircase, about three blocks from here," replied Macaroni.

"Part of the neighborhood," declared the President. "And this Club, as you may know, has been founded for the purpose of becoming a center of activities for neighborhood cats."

"Please, Mr. President, may I join the Cat Club?" begged Macaroni.

Sinbad and The Duke, who had been listening carefully from the visitors' row, called out: "Mr. President, don't worry. We'll bring him to and from the meetings until he learns to cross the streets by himself."

"Thank you, Sinbad and The Duke," said the President.

"The pleasure will be ours," said they.

Macaroni again begged the President to be allowed to join the Cat Club.

The President said, "Let me first explain to you our Rules and Obligations."

Sinbad and The Duke thought to themselves, "There goes Old Windbag." But they listened patiently while he droned his well-known words, "The principal Rule is that a member should possess some special talent or knowledge."

"I can dance," cried Macaroni. "Please, sir, may I join the Cat Club?"

The President replied, "I must also make clear to you that the principal Obligation of a member is to be willing at all times to contribute his special talent or knowledge for the benefit of the other members."

"Mr. President, I'll dance for you at any time. May I dance for you now?"

"Yes, Macaroni," said the President. "Show us a sample of what you can do. It need not be much. The Club gives a high mark for effort."

"No effort, sir, no effort," cried Macaroni. "I already know the Patpaw Polka."

The young dancer rose on his hind legs and capered through his steps so gracefully that Sinbad and The Duke nearly burst with

pride. And when he had finished, they glanced about the meeting ground and saw with pleasure that all cats there, including the President, seemed agreeably surprised by the youngster's fine performance.

"He's in," thought the buddies. And they expected to hear the President make the announcement.

But all the President said was, "Macaroni, please be seated next to Solomon."

The youngster did as he was told.

The President then cast an eye around the meeting ground and said, "The question is, shall the fancy dancer, Macaroni, be invited to join the Cat Club? Members shall cast a Yes vote by raising a right front paw."

Sinbad and The Duke each raised a right front paw and flapped it wildly.

"I'm sorry that visitors are not allowed to vote," said the President in a firm but not unkindly voice.

"Wither his tongue," thought Sinbad and The Duke, who felt they had a right to vote for Little Mac—their Little Mac. But they obeyed the President and waited to see what the members would do.

Madame Butterfly and Solomon each raised a right front paw. And from the low bough of the tree, Secretary Concertina sang, "My paw says Yes."

"The votes have been counted," announced the President. "Macaroni, I have the honor to inform you that you are now a member of the Cat Club."

"Thank you, Mr. President," said Macaroni. And then the little fellow turned his face toward the visitors' row and thanked his two friends there with his shining eyes.

Such was the joy of Sinbad and The Duke that they could no longer sit still. Sinbad drove a hard right hook to The Duke's jaw. The Duke delivered a similar hard hook to Sinbad's jaw.

"Attention, please," called out the President. "Will our visitors please control their paws?"

Sinbad and The Duke stopped their rough boxing and sat still.

The President now turned to Solomon and said, "Will our Wise One please favor us with a weather forecast?"

The wizened old yellow cat glanced at the sky, twitched his red whiskers, and squeaked, "Tomorrow night will be fair."

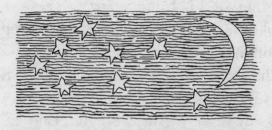

"Thank you, Solomon," said the President. And then, addressing the whole Club, he said, "We shall meet tomorrow night at this maple tree. At that time we shall discuss plans for the Club's first fun-and-frolic party. The program will offer not only music and riddles, but a fancy dance to be performed by our newest member, Macaroni. I wish that the program might also include a contribution by two members who could entertain us with a round of boxing—I mean soft boxing."

The President looked at the two visitors, as if hoping to hear from them that they

would like to tone down their style of boxing and become members. But their old
hatred of the President swelled within them
and they said nothing.

"This meeting is adjourned," declared the
President.

The President rose and walked from the
meeting ground and, by his manner, indicated that he wished no loitering in the
garden. So, while the other members headed
each for his or her own garden house, Sinbad and The Duke led Macaroni to the
garden fence. But they kept him there a
moment, because a light was shining in the
upstairs window of the vine-covered house.

"Little Mac," they said, "a man lives in that house. He's the master of this garden. Some night maybe you'll see him at the window."

"What's he like?" asked Little Mac.

"Very tall and very kind," said they.

After that they took Little Mac to his doorway and told him not to leave it.

"I'll wait right here until my master comes," he promised.

Then Sinbad and The Duke hurried toward their own house. They hurried because they felt a return of an old fear. It was the fear that the President was pursuing them in the hope of nabbing them and pulling them into his Cat Club and keeping them trapped with its Rules and Obligations. However, once the buddies were safe inside their house they quite forgot this fear.

Three Nights of Rain

For the next few nights, Sinbad and The Duke washed themselves and took Little Mac to and from the meetings of the Cat Club. While a meeting was in session, the two buddies sat quietly in the visitors' row and listened carefully to what happened. They listened at first because they wished to make sure their Little Mac received good treatment. They had no complaints.

And now that Little Mac was a happy member, the Club itself was beginning to make sense to Sinbad and The Duke. They could even see a meaning in the President and his Rules and Obligations. The President kept his paw on developments and prevented the Club from falling apart.

Tonight's meeting, for example, concerned the fun-and-frolic party which would be held in the near future, right here on the meeting ground beneath the maple tree. Most of the talk was what the President called an "open discussion." That is, everyone, except the visitors, could give opinions concerning the party's events. But the members, even the best-behaved of them, grew excited and talked out of turn or at the same moment. Tonight's meeting was turning into a babble of voices.

"Silence," ordered the President. "I have heard all your thoughts. I myself shall put the final touches to the program and present it for the membership's approval at the next meeting. Solomon, do we meet tomorrow night?"

The wizened yellow Wise Cat glanced at the sky. "No, Mr. President," he squeaked. "We shall have three days and nights of rain."

Sighs of disappointment rose from the membership. But the President said, "Let us turn the bad weather to good advantage. And while it rains, let each member practice his or her own special contribution to the party's program. I shall expect the very best in music, dance, and riddles."

The President looked toward the visitors' row and added in a pleasant voice, "The party will welcome visitors. I hope, Sinbad and The Duke, that you will come."

"OK, Mr. President. We'll bring Little Mac and stay awhile."

Now, as Solomon had predicted, the rain did fall for three days and nights, and there were no meetings of the Cat Club. Sinbad and The Duke lived comfortably enough in the house of their own, where the roof did not leak and where they could box whenever

110

they pleased. And no matter how hard it rained, they always found a good supper waiting for them in their supper nook.

After supper, they would dash through the rain to Little Mac's house and hold a powwow with him in the dry place under the front staircase. Sinbad and The Duke enjoyed his company. But their excuse for going to see him was his traffic lessons. Little Mac, though he was a bright youngster, had made no progress in learning to cross the streets by himself.

So, on the first night of the rain, when the two buddies reached his house, they said to him, "We've come about your traffic lessons.

You really ought to shake your brains and learn."

"But I like to cross the streets with you," he answered.

"Mac," they said, "you're old enough to travel to the Cat Club on your own four paws. We're beginning to feel silly taking you there and sitting in the visitors' row like two old mama cats."

He looked at them with puzzled eyes and asked, "Why don't you join the Cat Club?"

"We have other things to do," they said. And they proceeded to refresh his memory about the traffic rules.

Next night, Sinbad and The Duke quizzed Little Mac about those rules and asked him, "What does the green light tell you? Does it tell you to go or wait? What does the red light tell you? Does it tell you to wait or go? Should you, or shouldn't you, watch on every side for cars?"

He answered, "I've forgotten. And besides, I like to go with you."

They said, "Don't be a baby. Try to learn." And they drilled him again on the rules for crossing a street.

But on the following night, which was the third night of the rain, Sinbad and The Duke found that Little Mac had once more forgotten all they'd tried to teach him.

He said, "Give me until after the fun-and-frolic party. Right now I'm busy thinking about the dance I'll have to do at it. But after the party, I promise you, I'll learn to cross the streets. I'll miss going with you. But of course, you'll have those other things to do."

"Little Mac, we'll find time to come around here to your house and chit-chat with you."

"But what about the rest of us?" he asked.

"The rest of who?"

"The Cat Club," he replied.

"Oh, we shan't be going to the Club—not after you can get there by yourself," they answered in a breezy tone.

But that night, after Sinbad and The Duke had reached their own house, they lay down on their sofa. And while the rain beat on the roof above them, they thought of the future.

Sinbad and The Duke began to feel sorry that after the fun-and-frolic party they would no longer see the Cat Club. They would miss Madame Butterfly and the smile that she often flashed at them. They would miss old Solomon and his wisdom. They would miss the sound of Secretary Concertina's claws as she scratched the records of a meeting in the bark of the maple tree. They would miss—believe it or not—they would even miss the President.

Captains

of the City Streets

On the first night after the three nights of rain, the moon and the stars came out. Sinbad and The Duke washed themselves and then left home to take Little Mac to the Cat Club. They found the youngster waiting for them as usual outside his house. His face was serious.

"What's the matter with you, Little Mac? You look seedy," they said.

"Oh, it's nothing, fellas. It's just that last night, after you left me, I was trying to think," he answered.

"About your traffic lessons, we hope," they said in a joking manner which they believed might cheer him up.

"Yes and no. But anyway, let's go," he answered gloomily.

So away went the three of them, and they were the first to arrive at the Club meeting ground beneath the maple tree. The two buddies deposited Little Mac at his place in the membership circle and took their own seats in the visitors' row.

Then Concertina, the Club Secretary, arrived, and her face, like that of Little Mac, was serious. She disappeared, without a word, among the leafage of the tree. Next came Solomon, the wizened, yellow Wise One. He was always serious, but right now he seemed graver than usual.

Sinbad and The Duke wondered, "What's the matter with them all? Guess the rain must have dampened their spirits."

And now the President was seating himself at the foot of the tree. He didn't speak to anyone—he seldom did before a meeting

—but his face wore a pleased expression.

"Rain must have agreed with him," thought the visitors. "But where's Madame Butterfly?"

Suddenly she came, like a puff blown by the wind, and said sweetly to the President, "I'm sorry to be late. It's because I was thinking."

The President did not scold her. He never seemed to have the heart for that. All he now said to her was, "Please be seated."

The lovely creature sat down in her place, which was beside him. She looked like a cat who had been hatching a scheme.

The President did not seem to notice anything amiss. He swelled his chest and announced, "This meeting will come to order."

Scratch! Scratch! went the claws of the Recording Secretary in the maple tree.

The President continued, saying, "This is a most important meeting of the Cat Club. For I shall announce what I hope is the final arrangement of the program of our forth-

coming fun-and-frolic party. All ideas for members' contributions to the program are your own. We have discussed them many times. All that I have done to your contributions, known henceforth as numbers, is to list them in good order. I have labored on this program during three long, rainy, sleepless nights. I trust that it meets with your approval and that we need make no further changes. I beg you now to listen, without interrupting me."

The President cleared his throat, as though to make sure his voice would carry to the visitors' row, and he announced:

PROGRAM OF THE FIRST FUN-AND-FROLIC
PARTY OF THE CAT CLUB
TO BE HELD AT THE CLUB MEETING GROUND
BENEATH THE MAPLE TREE
UNDER THE AUSPICES OF THE PRESIDENT
Number 1. Tune:
"Beneath the Maple Tree" tooted on the nose flute by Madame Butterfly
Number 2. Dance:
"Pitty-pat Waltz" performed by fancy dancer Macaroni

"Good," thought the visitors. "Our Little Mac gets second place. Not bad, eh what?" And the President went on to announce:

Number 3. Song:
"The Records Are True" sung by Secretary Concertina

120

Number 4:
Riddles, asked by Solomon the Wise
VISITORS ARE WELCOME

"Visitors," thought the pair in the visitors' row, "visitors is us. He's put us on the program." And they felt happy to be on it.

But next moment they felt otherwise. For the President had finished speaking, and no one stirred. And during this silence—this very strange silence—the two visitors began to feel that it was no fun to be dangled at the end of a program, like a tin can tied with a string to a cat's tail. How they wished they might be a real part of the party! How they wished one of the numbers might have been:

Round of Boxing, Boxed by the Future Champs, Sinbad and The Duke

Ah, woe! The President had long ago declared that their style of boxing was too rough for the Cat Club. But they liked to box rough. They had learned to box rough when they were very young tramps adrift on the city streets. And even at this dreary moment, if the President should say "Sinbad and The Duke, would you care to tone down your style and entertain the party with a round of soft boxing?" they would refuse.

"Rough boxing's our specialty," they thought. "We can't sing or dance or play a nose flute. We could never ask a riddle. Rough boxing's the only thing that we know how to do, and the President won't let us do it. So at the party we'll have to sit right here on our bottoms—in the visitors' row."

Madame Butterfly gave Sinbad and The Duke a smile, which seemed to say, "You wait and see."

"Wait and see what?" they wondered. "This meeting's gone dead."

The silence which had followed the announcement of the program continued. The President glanced in a stupefied way toward his right and left, as if searching in vain for a clue to what was wrong with the results of his three long nights of labor.

Look! Madame Butterfly was raising a paw. (A new rule for asking permission to speak.)

"Madame Butterfly has the floor," declared the President.

"Mr. President," she said in her rippling voice, "I'd like to change my nose flute number. Instead of the tune, 'Beneath the Maple Tree,' I'd like to toot 'Over the Fence and Far Away.'"

The President blinked and said, "My dear Madame Butterfly, our party is to be held right here, as in your tune, 'Beneath the

Maple Tree.' What would be the point of a tune like 'Over the Fence and Far Away'?"

"Mr. President," replied Madame Butterfly, "I too did some thinking during three long, rainy, sleepless nights. And what I thought was this: Our first fun-and-frolic party should be more than just a party on home ground, which is old stuff to us. I believe we should really celebrate by turning our party into an outing."

"But where could we go?" queried the President in a dazed voice.

" 'Over the Fence and Far Away,' as in my new tune," she replied, tossing her beautiful head in the direction of the tall board fence that stood at the far end of the garden.

The President gasped. "Madame Butterfly," he said in a weak voice, "how could we go out anywhere beyond the fence? Our membership consists of pets. Most of us have never been outdoors at all, except in this garden. Even Macaroni, who lives beyond the fence, isn't able to cross the streets without help."

"Mr. President, let Macaroni speak for himself," urged Madame Butterfly.

She gave Little Mac a flashing smile. He seemed perplexed as to its meaning. Then his face brightened with some sort of understanding, and he raised a paw.

"Macaroni has the floor," declared the President.

"Mr. President," piped the fancy dancer, "I could have learned about the traffic sooner. But I like to come here with Sinbad and The Duke. They know all there is to know about the city streets. Ask Sinbad and The Duke to take the Club somewhere on an outing."

Madame Butterfly gave Little Mac another smile. It seemed to say, "You guessed my meaning. Now let the others carry on from here."

Then Solomon the Wise Cat raised a paw.

"Solomon has the floor," said the President.

"Mr. President, the key word is 'captains.' Let me add that Sinbad and The Duke would make trustworthy captains for the outing and for the ever-after," squeaked Solomon.

Sinbad and The Duke did not know what "the ever-after" meant. They thought it must be wise-cat gibberish. But Concertina called down from the tree, "Mr. President, I've made a record of those words, 'the ever-after.'"

"Concertina," he said in a voice that had suddenly regained its strength, "write also that the President carries on from here."

Waves of excitement surged over the meeting ground. Sinbad and The Duke believed the excitement was for an outing. They quite forgot they were sitting in the visitors' row, where silence was the rule unless the President requested otherwise.

"Mr. President," they cried, "we know a good spot for an outing. Niftiest little park that ever was. We'd be glad to take the whole Club to the park and home again—safe."

"Thank you, Sinbad and The Duke," said he.

"The pleasure will be ours," they said.

"Sinbad and The Duke," he said, "the pleasure of taking the Cat Club somewhere on an outing might be yours. But as matters stand, it will not—cannot be. And the reason is that the Club cannot accept so great a favor from cats outside the membership."

"The old killjoy," thought Sinbad and The Duke. And they expected to hear cries of disappointment from the membership. But the members remained calm and said nothing, as if they put their trust now in the President.

"Of course, Sinbad and The Duke," he continued, "if you were members, you might take the Club somewhere on an outing and thus be a real part—a very important part— of our party. Why don't you join the Cat Club?"

"We like to box rough," they replied.

He said, "Let's forget the boxing. Let's talk about your knowledge of the city streets. Do you realize that such knowledge makes it possible for you to join the Cat Club?"

"Oh," thought the young tramps to themselves, "he's after us again. But all we want is to be a part of the party. We don't want to be a part of the Cat Club." And they wanted to say No to the President and his Rules and Obligations.

But Sinbad and The Duke felt that tonight was not like the past, when they had refused the President's invitation to join the Club. Ever since they'd been visitors, he had been quite decent to them. So now they'd have to be polite and give him a good reason for refusing. They'd have to tell him about their liking for the free and easy life. But the free and easy life was difficult to explain. And all they could do at this moment was to mumble, "Mr. President, what do you mean by our 'knowledge of the city streets'?"

Mr. President said, "I mean it makes you eligible for membership as the Club's Captains of the City Streets."

"Captains of the City Streets," thought the young tramps. And they felt that those were good words—bright words, to which a cat should not say No. But Sinbad and The Duke could not say Yes. So they did not reply.

Mr. President asked them, "Are you listening?"

They nodded.

He asked them, "Are you interested?"

They stammered, "Maybe."

He said, "Will you please step forward so that I may ask you a few questions for our records?"

The two visitors stepped forward to within a paw's reach of the membership circle.

"Closer," he ordered.

They moved closer and for the second time in their lives they stood face to face with the mighty one. But this time they could feel a warm glow spreading toward them from the membership.

"Sinbad and The Duke," said the President, "you are acquainted with the Club's general Rules and Obligations. Know, therefore, that your own Obligation would be to contribute your knowledge of the city streets for the benefit of the whole Club."

"Mr. President, that doesn't sound hard," they admitted.

"But, my young friends," said the President, "let me explain to you in detail what your duties would be. They would consist of more than just guiding the Club out somewhere on a party. I look forward to the ever-after and I can see our Club growing and growing. Some of the future members will come from beyond the garden fence. They might need your help in learning to cross the streets on the way to our nightly meetings."

Sinbad and The Duke thought to themselves, "It's been fun helping Little Mac. It might be fun to help some others." So they said, "Yes, Mr. President, we would help those other new ones cross the streets at night."

"Furthermore," continued the President, "as the Club grows, our activities will increase. Now and then you might have to do a bit of daytime work."

Sinbad and The Duke remained silent. They were thinking, "Daytime work! Oh, no. That would really put the jinx on our free and easy life."

But while the young tramps stood there

on the meeting ground, they suddenly had a strange feeling that their old free and easy life was slipping from them. They had outgrown it, and something new had begun to take its place. The something new was the Cat Club, and the companionship which the Cat Club offered made the free and easy life seem cold and lonely. But "daytime work" were heavy words, and a cat must move with caution.

"Mr. President," they said, "what kind of daytime work do you mean?"

He answered, "There would be messages for you to carry to those of us who cannot leave our homes. I mean important messages."

"Important messages!" thought Sinbad and The Duke. "Oh, now he's talking sense." And they had an excited feeling of a new importance of their own.

"Mr. President," they said, "maybe you've picked the right fellas."

"I must warn you," continued the Presi-

132

dent, "I must warn you that our important messages would sometimes have to be carried in weather that is rough and even dangerous."

"Dangerous!" thought the young tramps. And their excitement mounted while they imagined themselves doing brave deeds which no other members of the Cat Club could accomplish.

"Listen, Mr. President!" cried Sinbad and The Duke. "Rains, winds, snow, and ice couldn't stop us. We'd carry messages and do other errands just the same, and the pleasure would still be ours."

The President smiled and then addressed the membership saying, "The question is, shall Sinbad and The Duke be invited to join the Cat Club as its Captains of the City Streets? Members who are in favor will please raise a right front paw."

Madame Butterfly, Solomon, and Little Mac each raised a right front paw. Concertina sang from the tree, "My paw says Yes, Yes, Yes!"

Then the President said, "The presidential vote, according to our Rules, is permitted to remain a secret. But this is a very special occasion. This is a moment which the whole Club has long desired. Therefore I should like to state that my own vote was Yes. Sinbad and The Duke, I have the honor to inform you that you have been unanimously elected to membership in the Cat Club. You are now our Captains of the City Streets."

"Wow!" shouted Sinbad and The Duke. And their excitement rose so high that they began to box. They punched and pummeled themselves out from the meeting ground and halfway across the long, moon-dappled garden.

"Halt!" cried the President.

They halted, and heard him call to them, "The master of the garden is standing at his lighted window, looking down at us. Come back here, Sinbad and The Duke, and let

him see that you have joined the Cat Club."

The Captains of the City Streets returned to the meeting ground and seated themselves quietly, next to their Little Mac, in the warm, friendly circle of the Cat Club.

Another Talk
with Patchy Pete

Another spring had come to New York City.
Sinbad and The Duke were still members of
the Cat Club. They attended all its meetings.

Last night the Club had discussed the
final plans for the Annual Spring Outing in
the park, and the meeting had not ended
until dawn. Thus, in the morning, Sinbad
and The Duke were still asleep in the house
of their own when they were awakened by
a scratch on the doorstep. Then a pleasant,
rusty voice cried, "What, no doorbell?"

The buddies jumped down from the sofa and rushed to the doorway. There stood a friend from the past—the old tramp of the many-colored coat, whom they hadn't seen for about a year.

"Patchy Pete!" they cried joyfully.

"So you fellas haven't forgotten me," he said.

"Bet your whiskers we remember you, and the time we met at The Tramps' Last Stop—and how you told us where to find our little house," said the buddies.

"I see you found it," said he.

"Step into our parlor," they said.

Patchy Pete stepped inside. He hadn't lost his swagger, although he seemed a bit older and rather glad to seat himself on the dusty floor.

"I can't stay long," he began. "It's curiosity alone that brings me here."

"Where do you come from?" they asked.

"From The Tramps' Last Stop," he answered. "I went there for my annual spring bite of chicken à la king. Then, having got so far, I thought I'd poke around this little old neighborhood and see if I could locate you. My nose had no trouble in picking up the scent of the big paws of two buddies who travel together. Your paw prints are everywhere."

"How do you like our little house?" asked the buddies.

"Wither my whiskers, if you don't sleep on a sofa now! Crinkle my paws, if the open road hasn't lost a couple of promising young tramps."

"Oh, Patchy Pete, we're still tramps. We

still roam the streets. Hasn't your own nose told you so?"

He said nothing to this, but asked, "How's your boxing?"

Sinbad raised a big front paw and drove a hard right hook to The Duke's jaw. The Duke raised a big front paw and delivered a similar hard hook to Sinbad's jaw. The buddies then exchanged good jabs and punches, but kicked clouds of dust up from the floor.

"Enough!" cried Patchy Pete. "Your skips and shuffles disappoint me. I can see that the sporting world has lost its future boxing champs."

Sinbad and The Duke sat down. "We're out of practice," they explained. "We've had lots of other things to do."

"Things such as?" queried Patchy Pete.

"Oh," they answered, "just those little things that come up when you settle in a neighborhood."

"Obligations!" chuckled Patchy Pete. "I told you that if you lived in a house of your own you'd develop neighborhood obligations."

"There are a few," admitted the buddies.

Patchy Pete said, "Tell me about this little old neighborhood. It used to be a catless land. But as I passed through it on my way to your house, I found handouts—lots of handouts tucked in quiet spots by many thoughtful humans."

The buddies said, "The neighborhood has changed and now it welcomes cats. Wow! you should see the handout we two are given every night for supper."

Then they told Patchy Pete about their supper nook, which a retired sea captain ran especially for them. And they described last winter, when there was the blizzard and their little house grew so cold that they had to spend a few nights by the boiler in somebody's cellar. But even then, they found a supper always waiting for them in their supper nook.

Patchy Pete said, "Ah! one kindly human has changed the spirit of your neighborhood. What else is new in Little Old New York?"

"Nothing much," they answered. For they decided not to mention the Cat Club. They loved the old tramp of the open road, and because they loved him, they didn't wish to hear him laugh at their Club and its Rules and Obligations.

So the buddies tried to redirect the conversation by saying to Patchy Pete, "Tell us about your wanderings since last we met. Give us news of the open road."

"Alas!" he replied. "Life on the open road is not quite what it used to be. The streets beyond Little Old New York grow more crowded with cars and trucks, and the big new buildings rise higher and are more jammed together. Many old tramps feel down on their luck. And the young ones complain of no future. So you must tell me more about your pleasant neighborhood. Maybe you will hit on a story that will cheer me up."

"Patchy Pete, there's not much for us to say," they murmured.

But he gazed at them as if he meant to pull a story out of them. "Come, fellas," he said, "tell me why it is your little house needs dusting, but you yourselves look rather spruce. I mean you are more washed than when I saw you last. Why all the washing?"

"Oh, washing's just a—" they answered and then checked their tongues.

"Just a what?" demanded Patchy Pete.

"A Rule," replied the buddies.

"A rule of what?" urged the old tramp. And again his sharp gaze rested on them, as if it would not leave them until they had told him the truth.

"A Rule of the Cat Club," they stammered.

"Cat Club!" exclaimed Patchy Pete. "Skin me alive if I've ever heard of such a thing. What sort of nonsense is this Cat Club?"

"Patchy Pete, it isn't nonsense," they protested. "It's a center of activities for neighborhood cats. Don't laugh. The Club means a lot to Little Mac."

"Who is this Little Mac?" queried Patchy Pete.

"It's a long story," they objected.

The old tramp said, "You might take turns in telling it."

Thus, with Sinbad saying the first sentence and The Duke saying the next few words and Sinbad picking up where The Duke left off and so on, the buddies told the following story:

"Little Mac's a young pet cat . . . You should see him dance . . . You should hear Madame Butterfly play her nose flute . . . There's a President . . . And the Club keeps growing and growing . . . Last Christmas Eve the Captain's own new little cat, Jenny Linsky, joined the Club . . . Jenny was wearing her red scarf and skating on silver ice skates . . ."

"Silver ice skates!" echoed Patchy Pete. And he began to smile.

"Patchy Pete, don't laugh. Those skates were nifty, and if you knew Jenny and the Cat Club, you would never laugh," said the buddies.

"Fellas, I'm not laughing. I'm only smiling because I find enjoyment in your story. Please go on."

Then Sinbad and The Duke continued: "One thing or another at the Club has kept us two fellas busy . . . That's why we're out of practice with our boxing . . . We've had to carry messages . . . We've had to gather news . . . Oh, maybe we forgot to say we're members of the Cat Club . . . Elected unanimously . . . Wholly unanimously . . . To be its Captains of the City Streets."

"Captains of the City Streets!" exclaimed Patchy Pete. And then he grinned.

"Fellas, your story lifts my spirit," he declared. "I remember that when I met you a year ago at The Tramps' Last Stop you were down on your luck. But you didn't complain of having no future. You decided to do something for yourselves and find a house of your own. I warned you about neighborhood obligations. But you seem to have fulfilled such obligations and to have made something of your lives. Your story, as you told it, was well worth my trip to see you."

The old tramp of the many-colored coat rose from the dusty floor.

"Patchy Pete, don't go," begged Sinbad and The Duke. "Stay with us forever, and share our little house."

He shook his head and said, "Thanks. But I'm an old-fashioned tramp who loves the freedom of the open road."

They urged him, "Stay at least a little while, and we'll take you on the Club's Annual Spring Outing."

"Fellas," he replied, "next spring, if all goes well, I'll come back and let you take me on your outing. At present, an affair of the heart—a romance—pulls me toward the east."

Sinbad and The Duke accompanied him

through the bushes to the garden lookout.

"I leave you now for the open road," said he. "From here I shall walk alone, with the sun and the moon on my spine."

The young buddies watched the old tramp saunter to the corner of the block. There, as he was rounding the corner, he called back to them in his pleasant, rusty voice, "Good luck to both of you. And long may your Cat Club live!"

HARPER TROPHY BOOKS
you may enjoy reading

The Little House Books by *Laura Ingalls Wilder*

J1   Little House in the Big Woods
J2   Little House on the Prairie
J3   Farmer Boy
J4   On the Banks of Plum Creek
J5   By the Shores of Silver Lake
J6   The Long Winter
J7   Little Town on the Prairie
J8   These Happy Golden Years
J31   The First Four Years

J9   The Noonday Friends *by Mary Stolz*
J10   Look Through My Window *by Jean Little*
J11   Journey from Peppermint Street *by Meindert DeJong*
J12   White Witch of Kynance *by Mary Calhoun*
J14   Catch As Catch Can *by Josephine Poole*
J15   Crimson Moccasins *by Wayne Dyre Doughty*
J16   Gone and Back *by Nathaniel Benchley*
J17   The Half Sisters *by Natalie Savage Carlson*
J18   A Horse Called Mystery *by Marjorie Reynolds*
J19   The Seventeenth-Street Gang *by Emily Cheney Neville*
J20   Sounder *by William H. Armstrong*

J21   The Wheel on the School *by Meindert DeJong*
J22   The Secret Language *by Ursula Nordstrom*
J23   A Kingdom in a Horse *by Maia Wojciechowska*
J24   The Golden Name Day *by Jennie D. Lindquist*
J25   Hurry Home, Candy *by Meindert DeJong*
J26   Walk the World's Rim *by Betty Baker*
J27   Her Majesty, Grace Jones *by Jane Langton*
J28   Katie John *by Mary Calhoun*
J29   Depend on Katie John *by Mary Calhoun*
J30   Honestly, Katie John! *by Mary Calhoun*

J32   Feldman Fieldmouse *by Nathaniel Benchley*
J33   A Dog for Joey *by Nan Gilbert*
J34   The Walking Stones *by Mollie Hunter*
J35   Trapped *by Roderic Jeffries*
J36   The Grizzly *by Annabel and Edgar Johnson*
J37   Kate *by Jean Little*
J38   Getting Something on Maggie Marmelstein
        by Marjorie Weinman Sharmat
J39   By the Highway Home *by Mary Stolz*

J41   The Haunted Mountain *by Mollie Hunter*
J42   The Diamond in the Window *by Jane Langton*
J43   The Power of Stars *by Louise Lawrence*
J44   From Anna *by Jean Little*
J45   Apples Every Day *by Grace Richardson*
J46   Freaky Friday *by Mary Rodgers*
J47   Sarah and Katie *by Dori White*
J48   The Trumpet of the Swan *by E. B. White*

J49   Only Earth and Sky Last Forever *by Nathaniel Benchley*
J50   Dakota Sons *by Audree Distad*
J51   A Boy Called Fish *by Alison Morgan*
J52   If Wishes Were Horses *by Keith Robertson*
J53   In a Blue Velvet Dress *by Catherine Sefton*
J54   Game for Demons *by Ben Shecter*
J55   Charlotte's Web *by E. B. White*
J56   Stuart Little *by E. B. White*

J57   The Hotel Cat *by Esther Averill*
J58   Julie of the Wolves *by Jean Craighead George*
J59   The Witch of Fourth Street and Other Stories
        by Myron Levoy
J60   The Cabin on Ghostly Pond *by Marjorie Reynolds*

J62   The Mother Market *by Nancy Brelis*
J63   Hemi: a Mule *by Barbara Brenner*
J64   The Giant Under the Snow *by John Gordon*
J65   The Boyhood of Grace Jones *by Jane Langton*
J66   Bridget *by Gen LeRoy*
J67   Pilot Down, Presumed Dead *by Marjorie Phleger*
J68   Hog Wild! *by Julia Brown Ridle*
J69   Here Comes Herb's Hurricane! *by James Stevenson*
J70   Captains of the City Streets *by Esther Averill*
J71   Luvvy and the Girls *by Natalie Savage Carlson*
J72   Berries Goodman *by Emily Cheney Neville*
J73   It's Like This, Cat *by Emily Cheney Neville*

HARPER & ROW, PUBLISHERS, INC.
10 East 53rd Street, New York, New York 10022